P9-CEZ-393

PIZZA PARTY

•• THE CARVER CHRONICLES ••

— BOOK SIX —

PIZZA PARTY

BY Karen English

ILLUSTRATED BY
Laura Freeman

Clarion Books
Houghton Mifflin Harcourt • Boston • New York

Clarion Books
3 Park Avenue
New York, NY 10016

Clarion Books is an imprint of Houghton Mifflin Harcourt Publishing Company.

hmhco.com

The text was set in Napoleone Slab.
The illustrations were executed digitally.

Library of Congress Cataloging-in-Publication Data

Names: English, Karen, author. | Freeman, Laura (Illustrator), illustrator.
Title: Pizza party / by Karen English ; illustrated by Laura Freeman.
Description: Boston ; New York : Clarion Books, [2018] | Series: The Carver chronicles ; book six | Summary: Third-grader Richard and his friends are four days from earning a pizza party for good behavior when a very strict substitute suspects that some of them have been cheating.
Identifiers: LCCN 2018033911 | ISBN 9781328494627 (hardback)
Subjects: | CYAC: Teachers—Fiction. | Schools—Fiction. | Friendship—Fiction. | Cheating—Fiction. | African Americans—Fiction. | BISAC: JUVENILE FICTION / People & Places / United States / African American. | JUVENILE FICTION / Social Issues / Friendship. | JUVENILE FICTION / Humorous Stories. | JUVENILE FICTION / Readers / Chapter Books.
Classification: LCC PZ7.E7232 Piz 2018 | DDC [Fic]—dc23
LC record available at https://lccn.loc.gov/2018033911

Manufactured in the United States of America
DOC 10 9 8 7 6 5 4 3 2 1
4500740363

For Gavin, Jacob, Issac, and Idris.

— K.E.

For Griffin and Milo.

— L.F.

Contents

One

Stupid Is Not a Bad Word

The children of Room Ten (except Ralph Buyer, who's absent *again*) at Carver Elementary School are standing in line, ramrod straight, heads forward, mouths closed. They are waiting for their teacher to pick them up from the yard. It's Monday, and it's their sixteenth day of excellent lineup behavior. Four more days of perfect morning lineup behavior and they get to have a pizza party. Their teacher, Ms. Shelby-Ortiz, has promised them. And she always keeps her promises.

So they wait, arms at their sides, mouths empty of chewing gum, lips pressed together against conversation spilling out. Well, Richard can see Calvin Vickers rolling his shoulders every once in a while—which he can completely understand, because suddenly he's feeling a teensy bit antsy too.

Richard wishes he could run in place—just a little. It's hard to hold this very still posture. He sneaks a look at the main building's closed double doors. The doors Ms. Shelby-Ortiz usually comes through when she picks them up from the yard. Most of the teachers have already picked up their classes and are walking back in that direction at the front of their lines. But nearly all of those lines are loose lines, Richard notes.

Not straight. Not quiet. Not everyone keeping their hands to their sides. He sees Montel Mitchell yank the hem of Brianna's jacket. She turns around and yells something at him, and their teacher just keeps walking them toward the main building like she doesn't even notice.

Richard lets out a tiny laugh. He's pleased that Room Ten's line has outshined all other lines for the past sixteen days. He's pleased that he's done his share. The slight smile on his face freezes when he suddenly hears hissing behind him. It's Yolanda.

"What are you *doing*?" she whispers.

“Nothing,” he whispers back.

“You’re not standing perfectly straight and I can hear you laughing about something.”

He straightens up. “I am too standing perfectly straight.”

This catches Miss Goody-Goody Antonia’s attention and she says to him in a voice slightly louder than a whisper, “You’re not supposed to be talking. Will you two please just *shut up*!”

Now Carlos, in front of her, jumps in. “Ooh, you said a bad word!” He turns practically all the way around to make his point face-to-face.

“I did not say a bad word,” Antonia counters in her normal voice. “It’s only a bad word at school. Nobody outside of school thinks *shut up* is a bad word.”

Deja joins in, but she keeps her head forward and her voice low. "We are at school. So shut up *is* a bad word."

"And *stupid*," Nikki adds. "Don't forget about *stupid*."

"Not in the regular world," Antonia replies. Then she lets go with a long, long sigh, closing her eyes and leaning her head back a bit, as if exercising extreme patience with her classmates.

"It's not *stupid* by itself that's a bad word. C*alling someone* stupid is what makes *stupid* a bad word," Nikki says.

Carlos looks toward the main building's closed doors and then says in a loud voice, "Would you all just be quiet! We're going to lose the pizza party!"

That stuns everyone into silence. They adjust their postures and look straight ahead, returning to their perfect lineup behavior. Then, way across the yard, they see the main doors open. It's not Ms. Shelby-Ortiz, Richard is surprised to see. It's Mr. Blaggart, the sub they'd had when Ms. Shelby-Ortiz broke her ankle.

He was *mean*. It had seemed like he was their punishment for driving away their first sub, Mr. Willow—who was way nicer.

Richard remembers some of their bad behavior. It had been Carlos's idea to skip around while he was reading out loud. And Ayanna was the one who decided to read in a voice so low no one could hear her. He's not sure whose idea it was for a bunch of kids to have a coughing fit during silent reading, but it was definitely Rosario who'd told everyone to sit wherever they wanted. And to keep switching names so poor Mr. Willow could never learn them.

The last straw—after the class's coughing fit—had come after lunch. Another teacher must have told Mr. Willow about the "Kick Me!" Post-it Carlos had stuck on the back of his sportcoat when he went up to ask him a question about the Social Studies assignment.

Poor Mr. Willow. He finished out the day, but he did not come back. That's when Richard felt extra guilty. Mr. Willow didn't deserve to be treated like that.

The next day, they'd had Mr. Blaggart. Former drill sergeant, current mean, mean, super-mean substitute teacher. Richard sighs. He wants to say something to Gavin, who's three people ahead of him in line, but knows he'd better not.

● ● ●

You can hear a pin drop as the class enters Room Ten. There's a list of their names on the whiteboard with a series of tally marks next to each. Richard looks at Gavin. Gavin shrugs. "I think we have to not get any of those tally marks erased. You have to keep as many as possible," he whispers.

Richard thinks about this. "He didn't do that last time."

Those who have permission to bring their backpacks to their desks to hook onto the backs of their chairs head to their tables. Those who Ms. Shelby-Ortiz has decided can't be trusted to have their backpacks within reach place them in their cubbies. Then they find their seats. Richard has to—*temporarily*—leave his backpack in his cubby. The week before, Ms. Shelby-Ortiz caught him with a toy in his desk.

"Wonder where Ms. Shelby is?" Carlos whispers to Richard before he heads to his desk with his backpack. *Not fair,* Richard thinks. The toy was Carlos's.

He'd let Richard "see" it right before line-up, and Richard hadn't had a chance to give it back.

"Yeah. Where *is* she?" Richard mumbles to himself. He looks around. And where is Khufu? He doesn't even know yet that Room Ten has a sub. And not just any sub.

Suddenly the shrill blast of a whistle interrupts the hushed silence. Everyone freezes in place. Richard and Carlos exchange looks.

"This getting into your seats and taking out your journals and getting started writing is taking too long." Mr. Blaggart looks around the room, then walks over to the board. "Obviously this class does not remember my rules. Let's go over them again. Notebooks out, and I'd better see a pencil in everyone's hand."

Richard notices Yolanda exchange looks with Deja, but they keep their mouths closed. Yolanda writes something on a piece of paper, folds it, then drops it to the floor at her feet. With one foot she passes it across the floor to the area under Deja's desk. Deja puts her foot on the folded paper. She waits a bit, then reaches down and palms it. Then puts it in her desk. She opens it with one hand, reads it, looks back at Yolanda, and nods. Richard wonders what's in the note.

Mr. Blaggart's loud voice interrupts Richard's thoughts again. "Now for my rules." He turns and smiles at the class, but it's not a real smile. It's a warning smile.

Richard reaches into his desk for his pencil, but he can't find it. He feels around and comes across wads of balled paper, stray crayons, and . . . Oh, there are the scissors the kids at his table had been looking for last Friday when they had Art. The box that held the table's common art supplies—scissors, markers, crayons, glue sticks—had been missing a pair of scissors.

Now he quietly returns them to the box and hears Yolanda whisper, "You're the one who had the scissors. I knew it."

"I *accidentally* had them."

Mr. Blaggart looks over at their table and homes in on Richard. "Do you have something you want to share with the class?"

"Sir?" he remembers to say from the last time the class had Mr. Blaggart as a sub.

"I see you're busy talking and not writing. Why is that?"

Richard doesn't know how to answer that question. Luckily, he doesn't have to, because just then Khufu enters the classroom with a note in his hand.

Mr. Blaggart looks over at him and frowns.

"I'm late because my father had a flat, and I had to walk when I hadn't been expecting to walk," Khufu says right away.

Didn't Khufu use that excuse last week? Richard thinks.

Beverly's hand shoots up, but she manages to keep her mouth shut until Mr. Blaggart nods at her.

"Mr. Blaggart, Khufu said his dad had a flat tire just last week." She looks around quickly for those who'll back her up. Several girls nod in agreement. Richard notices none of the boys is seconding this. And while everyone's attention is on Khufu and Mr. Blaggart, Richard, in a whisper, says, "Gavin, I need a pencil." Gavin looks at Mr. Blaggart while reaching into his desk. He passes one to Richard.

Two
Some Thoughts about Rules

Richard hurriedly writes the date on his first clean page. He quickly copies what Mr. Blaggart has already written on the board:

1. *Always address Mr. Blaggart with "Yes, sir," or "No, sir" when answering a yes or no question.*
2. *Place homework in the homework tray upon entering the class.*
3. *Complete assignments in a timely fashion.*

Richard frowns. He doesn't know what the term "timely fashion" means to Mr. Blaggart. To Ms. Shelby-Ortiz, it means by the end of the day. If you don't hand in your work with the rest of the class, then she has you work on it while the others have free time. It's best to stay on task.

"Is that true?" Mr. Blaggart asks Khufu. "You had a flat tire last week as well?"

Richard writes:

4. Stand when answering a question.

Then he waits for Khufu's answer, knowing he will come up with a doozy.

"We don't have much money, so my father's car is really old with really old tires."

Leave it to Khufu to come up with something that will make Mr. Blaggart sympathetic. He thinks.

"I'll be looking for a note from your father tomorrow. And don't forget."

Khufu looks perfectly calm when he replies, "I won't forget."

5. Requesting bathroom or water privileges after morning recess will result in losing lunch recess. Requesting bathroom or water privileges after lunch recess results in losing morning recess the next day.

6. No talking while working.

7. Free time activity—reading.

Richard starts to raise his hand, but then hesitates. Then he raises it all the way. Mr. Blaggart looks at him and nods.

"Mr. Blaggart, Ms. Shelby-Ortiz lets us work on the class jigsaw puzzle when we finish our work early."

"I'm not Ms. Shelby-Ortiz," he says simply.

Richard also wants to ask what the journal topic is, but now he hesitates.

As if reading his mind, Yolanda raises her hand.

"What is it?" Mr. Blaggart asks, turning to her.

In a small voice she says, "Um, can you tell us what the topic is for our morning journal?"

Mr. Blaggart frowns as if he hasn't even thought of a topic for the morning journal. He shrugs. "How about 'Why Do We Need Rules?' I think that's an excellent topic. Who agrees with me?"

Everyone quickly raises their hands.

● ● ●

Richard gazes at his blank journal page. *That's a lame topic,* he thinks, then quickly looks up at Mr. Blaggart as if the sub might be able to hear his thoughts. He finishes jotting down the rest of the rules and sighs. Not once has he ever given that topic any thought. He writes the date again on the next blank page in his journal. Yolanda, who sits across from him at Table Three, has already begun writing. He stares for a moment at her journal page. She notices and angles her journal away from him. She hunches over it.

Richard rolls his eyes. There isn't anything she's writing that he'd want to copy. He's pretty sure about that.

He writes the topic in the middle of the line. Then he takes a few minutes to ponder it. He glances at Khufu across the aisle from him. Of course, he's already dived in and hardly stops to take a breath as he writes and writes.

Richard turns back to his work, but then he

hears whispering. He might have missed it, except the whisper has a whistling sound. It's Deja, who sits across from Nikki at Table Two. Her loose tooth had come out the other day when she'd bitten an apple at lunch. Is she crazy? If he can hear that whistling sound, then surely Mr. Blaggart can hear it. Richard sneaks a look at the teacher, who's sitting at the front of the room behind his newspaper. He's leaning back in Ms. Shelby-Ortiz's special chair. Now he looks over the open paper and scans the classroom. "Who's talking?" he asks, squinting and peering around.

The class is silent. But then Richard can hear Deja whisper, "He likes to try and scare us."

"I'm waiting and I don't want to wait all day."

Deja slowly raises her hand.

"What's that?" Mr. Blaggart asks.

Deja looks. She has mistakenly raised her hand with the note in it.

Mr. Blaggart walks over to her, plucks the note from her fingers, and shakes it open. He scans it quickly while Deja looks down and Yolanda's eyes shift back and forth.

He clears his throat. "Let me see," he says. "What have we got here?"

He begins to read: *"Wonder if he has a wife? Wonder if he even has children? What kind of dad is he if he is a dad? Mean, probably. I wouldn't want him for my dad."*

Deja bites her lip.

"He probably doesn't even let them have dessert if they leave one crumb on their plates."

Richard hears a few stifled giggles behind him.

"Well, I'm thinking you two have already had your own personal recess," Mr. Blaggart says. "Am I right? You've been having a personal recess on your own—which means you'll be staying in when everyone else goes out for their recess. Am I clear?"

"Yes, sir," Deja remembers to say.

"Yes, sir," Yolanda quickly repeats.

Mr. Blaggart goes back to the front of the classroom and asks, "Why do we need rules?"

A few kids raise their hands, and Richard thinks: Why *do* we need rules? Everywhere you go there are rules. Rules for riding your bike: don't ride against traffic, wear a helmet, give cars the right of way. (Well, *of course* for that last one.)

His mother has lots of rules too. In fact, she's the family rule maker. She even has rules for his father: If he's first to get home, he has to pull into the garage and not just leave his car in the driveway, making it hard for her to squeeze by. Everyone in the house—Richard, his three brothers, and his dad—should load their dishes into the dishwasher as soon as they finish using them. Dirty clothes should be put in the clothes hamper immediately.

Richard sighs and stares at his blank page with the title positioned in the exact middle of the first line. Then he begins.

Why Do We Need Rules?

The whole wide world needs rules. Otherwise people would just not get along. We have to have rules when we drive our cars. What if no body followed the rule of stopping on a red light. All the cars would crash into each other and people would get really hurt. And what if people didn't get to the side of the street when a fire truck was going by. They might get smashed by the fire truck and what if all the kids ran in the halls. Kids would knock each other over and kids would get hurt bad. And what would happen if nobody put their cart away in the parking lot in front of Big Barn Supermarket? Cars wouldn't be able to drive around the parking lot and find parking. And what if you didn't keep your mouth closed when you chewed your food. That would be so yucky everyone would throw up at the table and that would be a big mess for your mother to have to clean up. We need rules so people don't get hurt and people don't throw up.

Richard stops there. He thinks he's made a good case for rules. He looks around. Half the class have taken out their Sustained Silent Reading books. Seven or eight kids are still writing in their journals, a few are reading their Social Studies books. Richard has a choice—if you can call that a choice. He takes out his SSR book. It's about a boy who gets lost on a camping trip and learns how to survive on his own before being rescued. Richard likes to imagine himself as the boy.

"Looks like most are finished with their journals," Mr. Blaggart says. "How about someone volunteer to share?"

The class is absolutely silent. Richard wants to raise his hand, but then he hesitates. Maybe his isn't as good as he thinks it is. And maybe Mr. Blaggart would bench him for writing a lousy journal entry.

Khufu raises his hand.

"I'd like to read mine, Mr. Blaggart."

"Fire away, Khufu."

Khufu stands and looks around at his classmates. "My entry is entitled 'Good Rules/Bad Rules: Why We Need the Good and Not the Bad.'"

Richard feels fear in the pit of his stomach. What is Khufu doing? Richard glances around. Antonia seems like she's stopped breathing. Gavin's mouth is hanging open, and Yolanda is looking back and forth between Khufu and the teacher.

Khufu clears his throat and begins. "Everyone knows that people need rules. If we didn't have traffic rules, cars would run into each other and people would be hurt or . . ." He pauses and then continues, "killed."

Antonia gives a little gasp.

Richard frowns. This sounds a lot like his own journal entry.

Khufu continues. "But some people like to make rules just because they want to make rules. Then people have a hard time following them because there are too many. There are so many that it's hard to remember them all. People who make a lot of rules would not like having a bunch of rules to follow themselves. They probably would be the first to complain about too many rules. Rules are good to have to keep people safe. But too many rules are too many."

He stops and sits down. The classroom is quiet. People are staring at Khufu, then looking at one another. Richard can almost feel them holding their breath.

"Well," says Mr. Blaggart. "That's . . . certainly an interesting take on rules."

Richard breathes a sigh of relief. It almost feels like Khufu has scored a point over Mr. Blaggart. He chances a look at Khufu. He dares not look at Mr. Blaggart or the long list of rules he has written on the board.

"Take out your reading texts and reread the last selection," Mr. Blaggart says, and returns to Ms. Shelby-Ortiz's desk to finish reading the morning paper.

After a few minutes, Beverly raises her hand. When Mr. Blaggart finally sees her, she begins, "Mr. Blaggart . . ." She hesitates, then looks down. "Never mind," she says eventually.

Deja's hand shoots up, and Mr. Blaggart calls on her. "Mr. Blaggart, what Beverly wants to know is . . . When is Ms. Shelby-Ortiz coming back?"

"I have no idea," Mr. Blaggart answers.

Three

Not Ms. Shelby-Ortiz

Finally the bell rings. Everyone puts away their reading texts and sits with their hands folded.

Minutes pass. Mr. Blaggart takes out a thermos from a bag sitting on the floor next to Ms. Shelby-Ortiz's desk. "Open your journals to what you've written," he says. He frowns at the class. "I've been thinking about what Khufu said about rules. Now I want to know what *you* think about what he said. Write a paragraph giving your opinion. Turn it in to me, and then you can go to recess.

Richard can't believe it. They're all going to miss recess! He needs recess. He'd been looking forward to playing basketball again like they had on Friday.

He'd had a good game, making baskets and surprising himself.

He opens his journal and begins his paragraph, remembering to indent.

I agree with Khufu. You don't want too many rules. Because a person just can't follow too many rules. Sooner or later they're going to start breaking one or two, probably on purpose. Too many rules makes people mad and . . .

And . . . what? He needs at least two more sentences to make a paragraph. He thinks hard, then writes:

They'll think what's the use?

He changes "think" to "feel like," which gives him an extra word. He goes back and adds "to have" between the words "want" and "too."

He reads it over. *One more sentence,* he thinks. *I need just one more sentence.* Finally, something comes to him:

But still it's better to have rules than no rules at all.

Richard stares at his paragraph. It sounds kind of stupid, but that's all he has on such short notice when he hadn't thought he'd have to write one more word on such a boring topic.

He stands to turn it in just as Nikki stands to turn hers in. Then they both freeze and quickly sit back down. Neither has gotten permission to stand up. *But there's no rule against it,* Richard thinks. Still, it just feels wrong. Nikki raises her hand and so does Richard. It takes forever for Mr. Blaggart to notice. He eventually lifts his head from his newspaper and nods at Nikki. Which is okay, because she has the same question Richard does: Can they turn in their paragraphs and go out to recess?

"Mr. Blaggart, can me and Richard turn in our paragraphs now?"

"Just put them in the basket," he says, going back to his newspaper.

Nikki and Richard look at each other. Richard keeps his hand raised. He has to hold it up a long time, because Mr. Blaggart just isn't noticing him. He glances at the clock. Only ten minutes of recess left. Finally, Mr. Blaggart looks up. "Something else?" he says.

"Can we go to recess?"

"What did I say?" Mr. Blaggart asks.

"You said after we write our paragraphs we can go to recess."

"Then you may go to recess."

Richard and Nikki put their journals in the basket and walk out as quickly as they can without running. A few other kids follow suit.

● ● ●

Once on the yard, Richard takes in a big breath of freedom. That was easy. The problem is, by the time they make it to the basketball court, recess is almost over.

Mr. Blaggart does let Deja and Yolanda out right at the end of recess to take care of restroom and water. As soon as they're spotted, Richard and several other students from Room Ten rush over and pepper them with questions:

"Did he have you guys stand on one foot the whole time?"

"Did you have to put your nose in a circle on the whiteboard?"

"Did you have to balance the dictionary on your head?"

"Wonder if he has a paddle?" Rosario asks. "Kids used to get paddled at school a long time ago."

The group is silent. Then Antonia informs them, "That's against the law now. But my great-grandmother told me that when she was a girl you could get hit on the hand with a ruler if you got an answer wrong."

"Wonder if Mr. Blaggart got paddled at school when he was a kid?" Nikki says. Then her eyes get big and she and Deja and Rosario burst into laughter. Soon there's laughter all around.

"That's why he's so mean," Yolanda decides.

Then before Richard knows it, the bell is ringing for everyone to line up.

"Thanks, Khufu," he says sarcastically as Khufu takes the basketball out of his hands. Khufu is ball monitor for the week.

"What do you mean, 'thanks'?"

“Mr. Blaggart had us write that paragraph because of what you said about rules.”

“But what I said is true.”

“You don’t have to say every true thing. And he thought you were talking about *him*.”

“I was.”

“You can’t do that with teachers,” Richard explains.

“Yes, you can,” Khufu says, and turns toward Room Ten’s lineup area. He bounces the basketball once, as if to emphasize his point.

In line, it seems Nikki has the inside scoop. She tells those around her that when she took the lunch count to the office, she overheard Mrs. Marker tell one of the second-grade teachers that Ms. Shelby-Ortiz is out with the flu.

“That’s better than a broken ankle,” Deja says, her eyes on the double doors. “She’ll probably be back in a couple of days.”

That gives Richard hope. Then they can go back to working toward their pizza party. He feels better already. But then he frowns. If Ms. Shelby-Ortiz doesn’t get over her flu soon, does that mean no pizza party? Will they have to start all over with being super, super good in line? Is that even possible? What if they have to be super, super good all the way until the end of the school year?

Then, after recess, Deja breaks one of Mr. Blaggart's rules. She accidentally answers a yes or no question without attaching *sir* to it.

Mr. Blaggart just walks over to the list of their names on the board and erases a tally mark next to Deja's. She stares at her shortened line of marks. It seems like she can't pull her eyes away. Mr. Blaggart turns to the class.

"In my report to your teacher, I'll be listing your names with a number beside each. That number will represent your tally marks. The higher the number, the better. I happen to know your teacher will be considering your scores when she decides if the class has *earned* a pizza party. If the score is below ninety, no party. Your score will include homework as well. So don't be the person who pulls the class down. Don't be the kid who ruins it for everyone else. It's on *all* of you to earn that pizza party."

He looks around the room, his gaze lingering on

a few of them here and there. Richard wonders why Mr. Blaggart's gaze lingered on him as well.

○ ○ ○

Now everyone is walking on eggshells, being super careful to stay on their best behavior. Richard checks the homework listed in a corner of the whiteboard. He closes his eyes and opens them again, hoping that some kind of magic would occur and some of that homework would just disappear. But no. There's Math, Spelling, Language Arts, and Social Studies. Ms. Shelby-Ortiz never gives all that homework. For Social Studies, they have to read chapter six and answer questions one to ten on page 92. That means they'll have to take that heavy book home. And his Math workbook, too, for the four pages of Math they have to do. It feels like a punishment. And for Language Arts, everyone has to outline their day. What does that even mean?

Antonia asks for clarification of the Language Arts assignment. Mr. Blaggart says something about breaking the day into time periods and labeling each one with a Roman numeral. Then they are to list events that happened during that time period: A, B, and perhaps C. Under each event, they should list a few details. Richard sighs.

During Math, Mr. Blaggart hands out a worksheet of multiplication problems with three place multipliers. Khufu dives right in. Richard doesn't know why. It's not as if he can do anything but read his Social Studies book or his SSR book when he finishes. So what's the point of finishing early?

Richard starts on his worksheet. This is going to take him all year. He's trying to concentrate when he feels something hit his cheek. It bounces on the floor, landing under his chair. He checks Mr. Blaggart, who's reading the paper at Ms. Shelby-Ortiz's desk again.

He reaches down to pick up the crumpled paper and catches Deja passing a note to Nikki with her foot. Whoever threw the note at him should have done it like Deja. Teachers nearly always catch a note being passed by hand. But they would never think to look under someone's foot.

Richard opens the piece of crumpled paper on his lap. It's a drawing of Mr. Blaggart. He looks around. It came from somewhere in the vicinity of Table One. Carlos, Beverly, Calvin Vickers, and Khufu sit at that table. But only Khufu is looking at him now. So Khufu must have drawn it.

In the picture, Mr. Blaggart is trying to lift a set of barbells with huge weights. His face is red and his teeth are clenched. He looks like a monster. Richard lets out a stifled laugh. He can't help it. Out of the corner of his eye he can see Mr. Blaggart looking around for the source of the sound. Richard holds his breath and gets back to his Math. Three place multipliers . . . Ugh.

Happily, Mr. Blaggart isn't zeroing in on him. But Richard is dismayed to see he's left the desk and is now sauntering around the classroom, stopping from time to time to check someone's work, making sure that person is on task.

When Mr. Blaggart bends over to get a better look at Carlos's math paper, Richard slips the drawing into his Social Studies book. He frowns down at it. He still hasn't gotten around to making a book cover. If Ms. Shelby-Ortiz was there, she would confiscate it until he brought in some kind of cover and showed it to her. Every textbook needs to be covered with something—brown paper or even newspaper.

Just then Antonia raises her hand and waves it around. Mr. Blaggart stops next to Richard's desk. Richard bends over his Math even more, feigning extreme concentration. "What is it, Antonia?" Mr. Blaggart says.

"Mr. Blaggart, I'm not understanding our Social Studies homework. Are we supposed to answer the question with information from the chapter, or are we supposed to get the answer from the Internet?"

Mr. Blaggart frowns. Then he closes his eyes as if he's searching for patience. Richard senses what Mr. Blaggart is going to do just before he does it. He takes

Richard's Social Studies book from his desk and flips to the table of contents. Then he flips through the pages of the chapter. Richard's heart beats fast. The note is tucked in toward the back of the book.

"Everything you need is right in this chapter. Look for the answers to the questions there. Simple."

"But I looked and looked and I still can't find the answer to number five," Antonia says, then adds quickly, "I'm finished with Math so I wanted to get a head start on my homework."

Just then there's a knock on the classroom door. Everyone turns to look. Through the door's narrow window, Richard sees Yolanda's mother. He knows what she looks like because she was at the science fair. Mr. Blaggart heads toward her. He deposits Richard's book on Ms. Shelby-Ortiz's desk, then opens the door and steps out into the hall.

Four

Leave It to Khufu

Richard's eyes are glued to his Social Studies book on the teacher's desk. He shoots Khufu a look. Khufu must have seen Richard slip the drawing into the book, because now he's got his hand clapped over his mouth as if he's trying to hold back laughter.

Mr. Blaggart steps back into the classroom. "Yolanda," he says. "Your mother is here to take you to your dentist appointment."

Yolanda's relief to be let out of class is easy to see. She gathers her things and is out the door in a hurry.

Mr. Blaggart claps his hands. "Okay. Now, where was I?"

Antonia repeats her concern. "I can't find the answer to number five on page ninety-two, and I've looked everywhere."

Mr. Blaggart picks up Richard's book again. He flips through the pages. The paper with Khufu's drawing slips out of the book and falls to the floor just as Mr. Blaggart looks up to ask Antonia to repeat the question number. Nikki opens her mouth to say something, but Richard vigorously shakes his head at her. She stops abruptly and gives Richard a puzzled look.

Luckily, the paper has landed mostly underneath the desk. A corner of it peeks out. Richard stares. If only it were completely under the desk. Mr. Blaggart is just the kind of person who can't let a piece of paper on the floor just be. He'll have to pick it up and deposit it in the trash.

He looks up to see Nikki staring at him. He must be looking scared. He feels scared. He takes a deep breath and closes his eyes for a moment.

"Funny," Mr. Blaggart says.

Richard quickly opens his eyes. Could Mr. Blaggart be talking about the drawing?

"I found the answer right away."

Antonia frowns.

"Check page eighty-three. Check it very carefully." With that he sits down behind the desk again.

Richard can barely take his eyes off that paper. He can't help but imagine different scenarios. What if the custodian finds it while sweeping the classroom and brings it to Mr. Blaggart's attention? Since Khufu was conscientious enough to label the note with Richard's name, Mr. Blaggart will know just whose it is.

Or what if no one finds the paper until Ms. Shelby-Ortiz returns, discovers it, and cancels all future pizza parties? No, that's too drastic. But what if she discovers who the culprits are (even though it should be just one culprit: Khufu) and tells them both how disappointed she is?

Richard *has* to get that drawing from under Ms. Shelby-Ortiz's desk before he leaves. He has to. It shouldn't be hard. He just needs to find a reason to go up to the desk. Then he'll use the foot trick to get the drawing. Khufu can be the distraction.

He glances at Mr. Blaggart, who's busy reading something on Ms. Shelby-Ortiz's computer. Richard checks the floor. Yes, the paper is still partially peeking out from under the desk, as if mocking him. Quickly, he writes a note to Khufu.

We need a reason to go up to Mr. B.
We need a question for you to ask while
I get the note. With my foot.

Richard folds up the note and drops it to the floor. He puts his foot on it, then coughs to get Khufu's attention. Khufu looks up and Richard widens his eyes and looks down at his foot. Khufu follows his gaze. Richard pushes the note toward him.

Khufu manages to get it under his shoe. He waits a few seconds, then reaches down to retrieve it. When he sits back up, Nikki is staring at him. "What are you guys up to?" she whispers.

"Why do you want to know?" He whispers back.

"I could tell on you," she says. "If I wanted to."

"But you won't, because I could tell Mr. Blaggart you have gum in your mouth. And some in your desk."

She scowls and goes back to her work, and Khufu places the note on top of his Math workbook page and smooths it out to read it. He whispers, "Let me take care of it." What's that supposed to mean?

Richard doesn't have to wait long. Khufu raises his hand. When Mr. Blaggart calls on him, he holds up his Social Studies book and asks Mr. Blaggart if he can show him something he doesn't understand. Mr. Blaggart nods, and Khufu marches up to his desk with his finger in between the pages to hold his place. He opens the book on Ms. Shelby-Ortiz's desk and points out something to Mr. Blaggart. Mr. Blaggart peers at the page and frowns. They have their heads together over the book for a minute or two, then Khufu turns to go back to his desk. As he does, Richard sees him deliberately knock one of Ms. Shelby-Ortiz's markers onto the floor and give it a little kick under the desk.

"Sorry," he says as he bends to retrieve the marker. He scoops up the drawing at the same time and stashes it in his pocket before returning the marker to the desk.

Richard didn't know he was holding his breath until he lets it out. Khufu gives him a big grin. *Leave it to Khufu.*

Five

What Does the Statue of Liberty Mean to You?

Luckily, by the end of the school day Richard still has all his tally marks. It's a first for him, being so good. At one point in the afternoon, he almost slipped and answered a yes or no question without including *sir.* But he caught himself just in time.

Right before dismissal, Mr. Blaggart saunters to the whiteboard with a sheet of paper in his hand. Most in the class stop what they're doing to watch. He consults it. Then he begins to add something to the long list of homework items. Rosario's mouth drops open. Richard's shoulders slump as he reads the new item: *Give the history of the Statue of Liberty. Then write what the Statue of Liberty means to you. No less than three paragraphs.*

He hates when he has to write something. There's no right answer like in math. And then your paper comes back with lots of red corrections. Then you have to rewrite it and include all those corrections. It's a lot of work. Especially when you don't have an opinion one way or the other because you've never, ever, ever even thought about the Statue of Liberty and you have to pretend that you have.

Richard sighs. Then he does a double take as Mr. Blaggart writes another item on the board. *Alphabetize your spelling words and put each in a sentence.* Is he trying to just totally ruin Richard's evening? Tonight is *Monday Night Football*—which he always watches with his dad and his three brothers. More writing? That takes time, and the rule in his house is no TV until all homework is completed—and checked by his mother.

And she doesn't just look it over. She asks questions. Especially if it's a writing assignment. She asks questions to make sure he understands the assignment. Then she asks questions to see if he has the appropriate information. She checks his grammar and punctuation and then has him go back again and again until it is written correctly and legibly, and—more important—until it makes sense. Sometimes he doesn't know that what he's written doesn't make sense until he's reading it to his mother.

He predicts that Statue of Liberty assignment is going to ruin his evening. It's going to take real *thinking.*

○ ○ ○

Richard's brother Darnell is sitting at the kitchen table licking chocolate off his fingers when Richard walks through the back door. He stops. He can't believe it! He marches to the cabinet beside the stove where his mother keeps her storage containers. The one in the back, in which he'd put the last chocolate doughnut—*his* chocolate doughnut, the doughnut he was saving to eat while he did his

homework—is gone! Richard straightens and glances in the sink at the empty plastic container.

"I was saving that, Darnell!"

"You can't have dibs on food!" Darnell counters. He grins his big, toothy grin and says, "First come, first served."

"That's not fair! That doughnut was mine!"

Darnell laughs. "The food in the house belongs to all of us." He pushes his chair back, gathers his book bag, and heads for the stairs to go up to the room they share. Darnell is in the fifth grade, but he usually gets his homework done quickly. Either his teacher doesn't believe in piling a lot of homework on kids, or he's just smart. Richard decides it's the first option.

He settles at the kitchen table and unloads his backpack, then gets up again to search the kitchen cabinets for a snack. Nothing. Absolutely nothing. He looks at the bowl of fresh oranges and apples sitting on the counter. They will just not do—not compared to a chocolate doughnut with chocolate icing. He's filled with disappointment.

Richard sits back down and takes out the math

worksheets. He's tempted to pull out his calculator, but he decides against it. His mom could walk in any minute and catch him, and then she would think he's a big cheater. He doesn't want his mom to think of him that way. He dives in without a calculator.

Since he knows how to multiply with three place multipliers it turns out to be kind of fun. He gets through his math homework in no time. Now for the stupid spelling words.

But first, he notices that there's a big family-size bag of chips on top of the refrigerator. He gets it down and pours some in a bowl. He's just about to start in on the spelling words when he hears his mother's car pulling into the driveway. Quickly, he shoves everything into his backpack, grabs the bowl, and carries it all up the stairs.

If he was at the table doing homework when his mother came into the kitchen, then she'd be sure to give him the third degree. She'd insist that he work on the writing assignment first. In fact, she'd set her purse on the counter, make herself comfortable next to him, and start guiding him through a brainstorming session. He didn't feel like brainstorming just then. He felt like playing a video game. Something like *Shadow World.*

In the privacy of his room—well, his and Darnell's room—he can do his homework and take breaks from time to time to play a video game. But to his disappointment, when he opens the door, there's Darnell sitting in the middle of their floor facing the TV with the controls already in his hands. Richard drops his backpack and settles on his bed with the bowl of chips to watch his brother. If he can't play, at least he can watch someone else playing.

Eventually, he takes out his homework. He's finishing his spelling just as his mother calls everyone to dinner. "And wash your hands before you come to the table," she adds. Richard hasn't gotten as much work done as he'd planned. He's been slowed by a few video games. He hasn't even thought of that Statue of Liberty thing he has to do.

At the dinner table, his mother turns to him and says, "So, what's your homework tonight?"

"Huh?" Richard had been listening to the sounds of the game coming from the television in the family room. His father and Darnell and Jamal have already finished their dinner and have excused themselves to catch the game. (Roland, his oldest brother, has football practice.) Richard just has to get through his peas, and he can join them. He's got his method. Fill up his fork, stuff his mouth, bite down once, then take a big gulp of milk.

His mother looks at him suspiciously. "I asked, 'What's your homework?'"

Richard takes another bite of gag-inducing peas. This time, it's two chomps and a gulp of milk. When he's finished, she's still waiting. In fact, she's put down her fork so she can give him her undivided attention.

"Math—done. Spelling—*done.*" He pauses here. "And I have to write a few paragraphs about the Statue of Liberty." He says that part quickly, hoping she doesn't notice it's a writing assignment.

"Let me see your first draft when you're finished with it," his mother says matter-of-factly.

The problem is, he hadn't planned on a *first draft.* A first draft implies a second or even a third draft. And that is just not the way he writes things—in drafts. Unless forced.

"Okay," he says in a small voice.

Just then a burst of cheers erupts in the family room. What did he miss? Something good, he's sure. He finishes off the peas and takes his plate to the kitchen sink. Then he races up the stairs to his room to get started on that stupid first draft.

This is what he comes up with:

I don't know much about the Statue of Liberty. It's always been around in NewYork and people like looking at it. And if you go to New york by boat, you get to see it and I think you can go inside and climb up a lot of steps to the torch. I think there are windows in the torch and you can look out and see boats and stuff in the water because the Statue of Liberty is on an island. I don't think there are any people living on that island because I have never seen any houses near the Statue of Liberty. I'm glad we have the State of Liberty because people who come to this country like to see it in person or see it from New York.

He reads his first draft over. Something tells him this is not what his mom has in mind. But maybe just this once she'll let this attempt pass and only go over the grammar and spelling. She won't send him back upstairs to his room to think. Really think. More cheers erupt from the family room. What's he missing?

Richard finds his mother in the kitchen, loading the dishwasher. It's actually Darnell's night, but he traded it for his mother's day on Saturday so he could watch the game.

She rinses and dries her hands while Richard looks toward the family room. He wonders what's going on in there. Suddenly, he hears his mother snapping her fingers. "Earth to Richard," she says. "I want your undivided attention." She begins to read while he watches her eyebrows furrow and her mouth sag at the corners.

Finally, she says, "Did you brainstorm?"

Richard has a decision here. Should he say he brainstormed when he didn't? He takes a moment, and then admits that he did not brainstorm.

"Go upstairs, research this—then *brainstorm*." She makes it seem so simple. But how's he going to brainstorm a subject he has absolutely no interest in? He hears another loud whoop from his dad and brothers. He hauls himself back upstairs, taking one last look at the closed doors to the family room.

● ● ●

Happily, when he finishes, his mom is on the phone with his grandmother. Richard knows she can't rush his dad's mother off the phone. He puts the paper on the Statue of Liberty in his backpack and slips into the family room. He eases himself down on the floor with Darnell, just in time for the fourth quarter.

● ● ●

The next morning, the students of Room Ten are back to perfect lineup while they wait for Mr. Blaggart to pick them up from the schoolyard. Where *is* he? Probably sipping coffee in the teachers' lounge. Maybe he hasn't noticed that the bell rang and that they're standing in perfect formation waiting on him.

The big double doors open and there's Mr. Blaggart, crossing the yard with a thermos in his hand. He looks like he might be in a bad mood, with those furrowed eyebrows, squinted eyes, and that mouth pursed into a hard-looking line. Richard stands extra straight.

● ● ●

The morning starts off just the way the previous one did. Everyone takes out their journals and checks the topic on the board. They dive in. Richard is surprised to see that Mr. Blaggart has come up with a new topic. "My Favorite Day of the Week." That's a great topic for Richard. He doesn't even have to ponder it. Friday is his favorite day of the week—especially when he's riding his bike home from school and he's thinking about the whole weekend ahead of him. It's easy to write on that topic.

After Mr. Blaggart has given them time to complete their journal entries, he says, "Okay, Khufu. You owe me a note. Where is it?"

All heads swivel to Khufu. He looks perfectly at ease. He pulls his book bag off the back of his chair and proceeds to rummage and rummage around in its main compartment, while everyone watches. Then he unzips one of the smaller pockets. Nothing. Richard can't help smiling. Already, Khufu's antics are entertaining. Richard looks over at Gavin and rolls his eyes. Gavin draws in his lips as if he's trying to keep from laughing out loud. Even Antonia has her hand over her mouth—Richard can tell she's got a smile behind it.

At last, Khufu unzips one of the side compartments and pulls out a folded piece of paper. Richard sits up with interest. This should be good. Mr. Blaggart takes the paper out of Khufu's hand. He shakes it open and studies it. He glances at Khufu and continues reading.

"Did your father write this note?" he finally asks. Everyone waits for the answer.

"No, sir," Khufu says. "I did."

A few kids gasp.

"And why didn't your father write this note?"

"He had to tell me what to write because he sprained his right hand and that's the hand he writes with," Khufu says.

"Your father has a sprained hand."

"Yes, sir," Khufu says.

"Yesterday a flat tire, and today a sprained hand."

"Yes, sir," Khufu says again.

"Read this note to the class."

Khufu takes the note and begins to read, while Mr. Blaggart listens with his eyes squinted and his mouth shoved to the side.

"Dear Mr. Blaggart, Khufu told me you wanted this note because you weren't sure I had a flat tire when I did have a flat tire. So that was why my son was late to school. He got up when I told him to get up and he got ready for school in time to get there on time.

But we had a flat tire and he had to walk when he

wasn't thinking he would be walking instead of riding. So I hope you know that I did have a flat tire and that was why he was late. I got a new tire so he will be on time from now on. Sincerely, Khufu's father."

"Let me ask you this," Mr. Blaggart says. "Did your father really dictate this note to you?"

Khufu nods solemnly.

Mr. Blaggart looks around the classroom. "How many think Khufu's dad dictated this note?"

Richard starts to raise his hand, but hesitates when he notices that the only people who have done so are Khufu's friends. Him, Calvin, Carlos, and Gavin. Then he thinks if he doesn't raise his hand, Khufu will probably ask him why. He raises it, and Mr. Blaggart turns to him.

"So, Richard. This letter sounds okay?"

Now Richard doesn't know what to do. He nods weakly.

"Okay. Good to know. I'm going to call Khufu's father during recess and find out."

Richard glances over at Khufu, surprised to see him looking perfectly calm. Maybe his father really did dictate that note.

Happily, at that moment the recess bell rings. Everyone clears their desktops, even if it means quickly stuffing miscellaneous items into their desks. Once that's done, most sit up extra tall in their seats with hands folded, waiting to be called on.

Surprisingly, Mr. Blaggart dismisses the class table by table with no further comments. Richard thinks he must be in some kind of hurry to get to the teachers' lounge. Maybe there's another teacher he likes who he's meeting there. The thought makes Richard laugh to himself as his table stands up and they head toward the door.

"Shhh!" Yolanda says. "You're going to make us lose recess."

Six
Girls Like Basketball Too

Outside, it feels as if they've been released from prison. Most of the boys go directly to the basketball court. Deja and Rosario join them.

"You guys have foursquare," Khufu says, passing the basketball to Richard. Richard pivots and tries to make a basket. The ball bounces off the rim.

"Room Ten has two areas this week," Deja says. "Which means we can play either one."

"What if everyone in the class decided to play basketball?"

Deja looks around. "That's not going to happen."

"Fine, then," Richard says. "We're not going to go easy. We're going to play our regular game."

"I *want* you to play your regular game. But me and

Rosario get to be on the same team," Deja says, pursing her lips. Richard shrugs. "Fine. We're still going to play our regular game."

So they do. Which means keeping the ball out of Deja's or Rosario's hands. As soon as Richard shoots and makes a basket, he elbows Deja out of the way.

"Foul!" Deja exclaims, surprising him. "I get a free throw!" She grabs the ball and dashes to the free throw line. The two teams take their places along the sides. Deja dribbles the ball a few times, then brings it to her chest and shoots. It bounces off the rim, to a burst of laughter from Richard's team. Gavin even jumps around in a circle.

"Girls can't play," he announces.

Deja ignores them and focuses on her second shot. She dribbles, brings the ball to her chest, and gazes at the net with squinted eyes. Then she shoots the ball in a perfect arc toward the basket. It goes in with a swish.

The boys are so shocked, they stay frozen in place while Rosario gets the ball and passes it to Deja. Gavin easily steals the ball away from her and dribbles it around the court until he can shoot. It bounces off the rim and lands near Deja's feet. As she tries to grab it, Richard elbows her out of the way again.

"You can't do that!" Deja protests.

"It's called *basketball!*" Richard yells as he passes the ball to Carlos, who shoots and makes the basket. Now it's four to one—in favor of Richard's team.

"That shouldn't count because you fouled!" Rosario says.

"Did not!"

"I watch basketball with my dad! I know when a person fouls!"

"But . . . you're a girl. So you don't even know what you're watching!"

Rosario opens her mouth to counter that, but no words come out for a few seconds. "You're . . . you're . . . That doesn't even make sense!"

Gavin dribbles the ball toward the basket, stops,

takes aim, and sinks the shot just as the bell rings for lineup.

"Whoo-hoo!" Carlos yells. "We won! We won, plus we knew we were going to win! 'Cause we're the best!"

"That's okay," Rosario says. "We'll get you at lunch recess. Kickball—boys against girls." She walks away.

● ● ●

Richard enters the class feeling good. Then he sees what's written on the board, and his heart drops. He remembers the sloppy job he did on the Statue of Liberty writing assignment. Maybe if he just doesn't make eye contact with Mr. Blaggart, someone else will have to go up and stand before the class to read what they wrote.

But after everyone is seated, Mr. Blaggart claps his hands once and looks directly at Khufu. Eventually, everyone is looking at Khufu.

"Well, Khufu . . . I'm afraid I couldn't get in touch with your dad."

"That's because last night he had to go out of town. I'm staying at Miss Lee's. She lives downstairs from us."

"And how is it you neglected to tell me this?"

"I forgot," Khufu says simply.

"You forgot."

Khufu nods.

Mr. Blaggart shakes his head slowly. "Take out your Social Studies books and turn to page one hundred twenty-two."

Once everyone has taken their Social Studies books out of their desks, Mr. Blaggart announces, "I'm looking for someone to share what they wrote about the Statue of Liberty."

Richard stares out the window. *Don't call on me. Please don't call on me.* He's hoping that just thinking this will keep Mr. Blaggart from focusing on him.

"Looks like I'm going to have to 'volunteer' someone." He turns to Richard just as Richard chances a glance away from the window at him. It's as if he knows that, more than anything, Richard does not want to read his homework on the Statue of Liberty.

"Richard," Mr. Blaggart says.

Richard sits there for a few moments while Mr. Blaggart goes through the papers in the homework basket. He finally plucks out Richard's paper. He hands it to Richard. It's as if Mr. Blaggart already knows that Richard did a slipshod job and he wants the rest of the class to know it as well. Richard gazes at the paper in his hand. Everyone stares at him.

He begins:

"Um . . . *I like the Statue of Liberty because it is for liberty. It's for freedom and people getting to come to America and . . .*" He squints at his writing. *"And . . ."* He can't make out what he's written. Ms. Shelby-Ortiz has told them over and over that the most important thing a person can do after writing anything is to read it over. You're likely to discover skipped words, misspellings, illegible handwriting, and a bunch of other stuff. But he'd been so anxious to be finished so he could see at least some of the *Monday Night Football* game, he hadn't bothered to look his work over.

He makes up something. ". . . And, uh, wanting to be free and find jobs and nice houses." Yes. He did sort of repeat a bit of his original writing—which he now thinks is better than when his mother saw it. He goes on reading, and when he finishes, it's quiet. Richard glances at Mr. Blaggart. Mr. Blaggart opens his mouth and closes it again. Finally he says, "Do you think . . ."—he pauses—"that your work reflects the homework assignment I gave you?" Richard feels his face grow warm. Mr. Blaggart points to the white-board. "Read what you were *supposed* to do. Out loud so everyone can hear it."

Richard reads, "Give the history of the Statue of Liberty. Then write what the Statue of Liberty means to you."

"Is that what you did?" Mr. Blaggart asks.

Richard doesn't say anything. He feels the eyes of his classmates on him. He feels their relief at not being *him*. Mr. Blaggart takes a book off his desk and walks over to Richard. "You may borrow this book, *What is the Statue of Liberty?*, and keep it overnight. You need to do this assignment again. I know you can do a better job." Reluctantly, Richard takes the boring-looking book while everyone keeps their eyes glued on him. "Oh. And I'd better not see any evidence that you've copied any passages from it," Mr. Blaggart warns.

Richard stares at the book. The cover shows just the top half of the Statue of Liberty—mainly the head and the crown and the torch. This is going to require *more* thinking—more than he'd planned on doing.

In his peripheral vision, he sees Antonia waving her hand eagerly at Mr. Blaggart. The teacher turns to her.

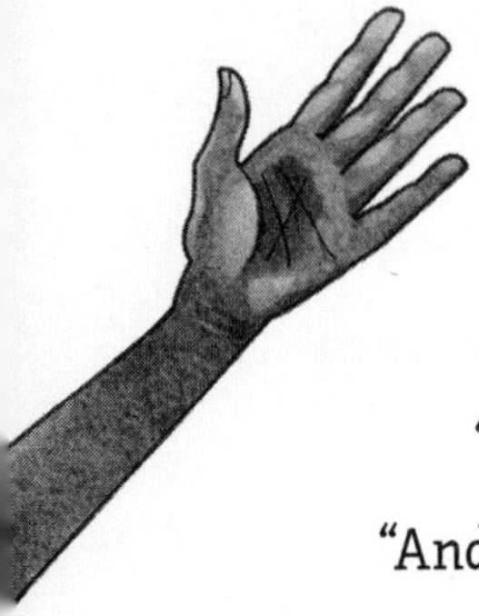

"Can I read mine, Mr. Blaggart? I made sure I followed what you wrote on the board. So can I read mine?"

"Take it away," Mr. Blaggart says.

"And I didn't copy, either. Everything is in my own words," says Antonia as she makes her way up to the front of the class—even though Mr. Blaggart didn't instruct her to do this.

He takes Antonia's paper from the basket and hands it to her. She positions herself in front of the whiteboard. *"First, I have to say that most people don't even know why we have a Statue of Liberty. I'll give you the definition of* liberty *first. And that means 'free.' Now, there were a lot of people in this country who were not free. Then they became free. And two Frenchmen were happy and impressed that America made these people free and even fought over it. One's name was Edouard Rene de Laboulaye."* She slows there to pronounce every bit of the man's name. Probably because it's French and long.

"And the other guy was named Frederic-Auguste Bartholdi. And he was the one who was going to make it. He was a sculptor. Does everyone know what a sculptor is?" She looks around.

Nearly the whole class looks bored enough to take a nap. There are a few moments of silence while Antonia squints at her paper. Finally she says, *"They make things, like, out of different materials and sometimes out of clay. So they wanted to put it on this island—right where it is today. And it was okay because the island belonged to the country and not the city of New York. They made the statue of a woman and that came from Libertas, the goddess of freedom. Some people think he made it*—this Bartholdi guy—*to look like his mother. She has a crown with seven rays and some people say it's for the seven seas or the seven continents: North America, South America, Europe, Asia, Africa, Australia, Antarctica.*

"The statue means a lot to me because it's about freedom and everyone wants to be free." Then she adds in a quiet voice, *"Because a long time ago a lot of people weren't free."*

Finally, she's finished.

"O . . . kay . . . " Mr. Blaggart begins slowly. It's as if he hasn't finished thinking about what Antonia's said, but it's time to say *something.* "Good job, Antonia. Good job. Uh . . . are there any questions for Antonia?"

Khufu is the only one who raises his hand.

"Okay, Khufu."

"I don't have a question," he says. "I have a statement."

There are tiny frown lines that grow on Mr. Blaggart's forehead. "Go ahead," he says.

"Well," Khufu begins. "I don't like the way the statue looks. I think her clothes are old-fashioned and her head is too big."

As he talks, frown lines begin to form on Antonia's forehead as well. "Her head is just right—for her body," she responds. "No one would want to see a little head on that big body."

"That would be scary," Nikki says under her breath. Luckily, Mr. Blaggart doesn't seem to hear her.

But then Antonia turns to Nikki and says, "It wouldn't be scary. It would be strange."

Mr. Blaggart steps in then. "Well, thank you, Antonia. I think we can move on now."

Moving on means more reading and answering questions in their Social Studies books while Mr. Blaggart reads the paper. Boring stuff. Richard can hardly wait until the bell rings for lunch.

Seven
I Got You Out!

Happily, PE is on Tuesdays. The first thing Richard had done when he walked into the classroom that morning was check the schedule on the whiteboard to make sure Mr. Blaggart knew that the class had Physical Education in the afternoon, at two.

Now, on his way to the lunch tables, he thinks about Deja's morning recess challenge. "Get yourself ready, 'girl team,'" he says as she passes him.

"You get yourself ready," she counters.

"Ha, ha, and ha!" Richard says. "That's so funny I almost forgot to laugh."

Deja doesn't have a comeback. She frowns as if she doesn't know what that's supposed to mean. Richard realizes it's something he's heard his mother say to his father. Something people must have said a long, long time ago, when she was a kid.

● ● ●

Nikki, Antonia, Yolanda, Rosario, and Keisha are on Deja's team.

Carlos, Gavin, Calvin, and Khufu are on Richard's team. The rest of the Room Ten kids are on the four-square court.

This is great, Richard thinks. *It won't have to take all day for me to get my turns at kicking.*

Deja wins the coin toss, so her team is up first. Gavin pitches, and Deja kicks the ball hard between second and third base. She easily runs around the bases. As she crosses home, she pumps her arm and yells, "Yes!"

"One to *zero!*" Nikki announces.

Richard finds that extremely annoying. Nikki's up next. Gavin is still the pitcher. Not good. Gavin rolls the ball way too slowly. Nikki almost has enough time to take a nap before the ball crosses home plate.

She kicks it all the way to the water fountain on the side of the main school building. It bounces off to the left and rolls across the schoolyard and right into Arthur Mason's arms. He's in Mr. Beaumont's class across the hall. They're out for lunch recess too and are playing sock ball on the other baseball diamond.

Everyone on Richard's team yells, *"Throw us the ball! Throw us the ball!"* But Arthur just stands there looking confused. Meanwhile, Nikki runs around the bases, dramatically stomping on each one and then sauntering across home plate as Arthur Mason finally throws the ball across the yard to Richard's waiting arms.

"Two to *zero!* Two to *zero!* Two to *zero!"* the entire girls' team chants loudly as they stomp around in a circle.

Look at them, Richard thinks, filled with disgust at their behavior—and a little bit of embarrassment that his team is losing as well. Some of the kids from Mr. Beaumont's class keep looking over at their game. He sees Dyamond Taylor pointing and laughing. He'll show them. Just wait.

Now Antonia is up. Gavin pitches the ball. It goes to the side of home plate.

Antonia watches it roll by.

"Strike one!" Richard announces.

"That was out," Antonia states.

"That was in!" Richard asserts. He looks around for people to back him up.

"That was in!" Calvin repeats.

"Do it over!" Rosa calls out.

They can't agree, so that's what they have to do. Gavin pitches the ball again—for some reason, a little slower than the first time. Antonia kicks it high and it lands right in Gavin's arms.

"Out! Out! You're O! U! T! Out!" The whole boys' team erupts with yells and fist bumps and running around in circles. Two more outs quickly follow. Finally, the boys' team is up. They charge to home plate and get in line, with Richard at the head.

"Give me space, boys!" he says, while doing all kinds of gyrations in preparation, including pretend-spitting on his palms and rubbing them together. Though he doesn't know why. Then he does that neck thing that boxers do.

Deja rolls her eyes and takes her place in the

middle of the diamond. Once everyone is where they're supposed to be, she pitches the ball. Richard stops it with his foot as it goes wide of the base. "Ball one," he says. "What's wrong? You can't roll it over the base?"

"I can roll it fine," Deja replies.

"Well, roll it then."

Deja pitches the ball again. It goes straight toward the base. Richard kicks it halfway across the yard and then he begins to run as fast as he can around the diamond. Nikki has dashed after the ball. She scoops it up and throws it to Deja, who now makes a mad dash to third base, bumping into Richard in the process.

"Out," she yells. "You're out!"

"I got there first. I put my foot on the base!" he protests.

"Did not! I got to the base first!"

"Ooh, ooh—you did not. You *know* you didn't!"

Now the girls' team quickly crowds around the situation at third base. For some reason, Richard still has his foot planted firmly on it.

"Let's just do it over," Antonia suggests.

Deja sighs and stomps back to the center of the diamond with the ball. Richard is barely ready when

the ball comes at him fast and hard. He turns in time to kick it toward second base. It rolls and rolls while Rosario goes after it. She doesn't get it in time, and Richard runs to first and second and then on to third. By the time Rosario gets her hands on the ball, he's crossing home plate.

But he didn't actually *touch* third base with his foot. And Deja saw it.

"One to two," Carlos calls out. "One to two!"

"*Zero* to two," Deja declares. "Richard's foot didn't touch third base!"

"It did so!" Richard counters.

"It didn't!" Deja says. "I saw that clearly."

"Then you can't see! You need glasses!"

There's nothing to be done after that, because the bell rings and Mr. Blaggart, who'd been sitting on a bench at a lunch table correcting papers, is on his feet, blowing his whistle.

Everyone lines up.

"Cheater," Deja whispers as Richard walks by. His eyes get big. He opens his mouth to speak. It's *Deja* who's the cheater! But he keeps quiet. Mr. Blaggart is looking his way, and he doesn't want to lose the pizza party.

● ● ●

"Get into your seats quickly," Mr. Blaggart says once they're back in the classroom. He deposits a stack of papers in front of Rosario. Antonia raises her hand.

"Mr. Blaggart, Beverly is homework monitor. She's supposed to pass out the homework."

"Well, Rosario is passing out the homework today. Anyone who has a problem with that can write a five-paragraph composition detailing their concerns."

Richard frowns. No one raises their hand.

Richard doesn't pay any attention to the homework until Rosario gets to his table. Then he looks at the packet she places before him and his mouth drops open. That's a lot of homework for one night. It must be for the rest of the week. He already has to rewrite his Statue of Liberty paper. How is he supposed to get all of this done?

Deja raises her hand. Mr. Blaggart nods in her direction.

"Mr. Blaggart, sir, is that for the rest of the week or is it just for tonight?"

Mr. Blaggart frowns. "That's tonight's homework," he says simply, then adds, "I want that completed by tomorrow morning."

More mouths are hanging open in astonishment. Beverly and Yolanda look at each other.

Antonia raises her hand. "Mr. Blaggart, sir, um . . . We usually get more time for such a lot of homework."

"And I know you can get it done. Then I'll be able to give your teacher a good report. I'm sure you want me to give your teacher a good report."

● ● ●

At the end of the day, Richard sits up extra straight so his table can be called first. That morning, he'd thought ahead and squirreled away two of the last of the chocolate chip cookies at home—this time in a

Ziploc bag in the back of the freezer behind the boxes of frozen vegetables. His cookies should be safe. But you never know with Darnell, and Jamal, too. They can sniff out sweets no matter where he hides them.

So now he's sitting tall in his seat with his hands folded, thinking about those cookies. The floor under his chair and his part of Table Three is clean. His desk is orderly, its top is bare. Mr. Blaggart has started patrolling the classroom with the pointer from the whiteboard in his hand—randomly peeking in desks, eyeing the floor, checking the tabletops. He nods at Table Three, Richard's table, and those who have to retrieve their backpacks from their cubbies carefully *walk* to them. Richard places his homework packet on top of the bank of cubbies, grabs his sweatshirt, and pulls it over his head. Calvin elbows him, and when Richard looks he makes a funny face. Richard almost bursts out laughing, but somehow he's able to stop himself.

Before he can even sit down again, Mr. Blaggart is calling on Table Three to line up. *Yes!* There's a good chance he'll get to his chocolate chip cookies before his brothers do.

Richard waits for Khufu and Gavin at the bike rack. Calvin is staying for band practice, and Carlos now stays for Afterschool Club. Richard still thinks Khufu's painted-over orange bicycle is ugly. He's glad—so glad—that he has his own blue-and-silver BMX.

They stay on the side streets where almost no traffic goes, riding close to the parked cars in a straight line. His parents have gone over and over the safety rules. Helmets are essential. If Richard's mother or father caught him not wearing his helmet, even once, he'd lose his bike privileges for a month. At least. So he's glad he has his helmet. He's glad he has his friends. He's glad he has his chocolate chip cookies in the freezer behind the frozen peas.

Eight
Where's My Homework?

When they get to Richard's house, Khufu and Gavin flop down on the porch to rest for a bit before they continue on.

Richard wants to ask Khufu if his father really dictated that funny-sounding note. But he doesn't. He's not sure Khufu would tell the truth. The bad thing about saying things that aren't true is that when you say something that *is* true, people might not believe you. Richard wonders if Khufu's father is actually out of town, too.

• • •

After his friends have ridden off, he goes into the kitchen, his mouth watering in anticipation. No one's there. Richard remembers that Darnell and Jamal are still at school. Darnell has Homework Club (which is really for those who tend to slack off when it comes to completing their homework assignments) and Jamal has Debate Club.

The house is *his*. He sets his backpack on the table, then remembers his mother telling him *not* to put his germy backpack there. He places it on the floor beside the chair, then goes directly to the refrigerator. He stands there a moment, imagining opening the freezer door, reaching past the frozen lasagna, past the packages of frozen spinach and broccoli and (ugh) peas, to his Ziploc bag of chocolate chip cookies. His mouth waters even more.

Finally, he opens the freezer door. He reaches back and feels around for the Ziploc bag. *Nothing.* He feels around behind the half gallons of ice cream. Nothing. He takes the big items out, gets the step stool, climbs up, and peers all around the freezer. *Nothing.* No cookies!

He can't believe it. He knows who the culprit is—but how did Darnell know they were there? He must have seen Richard putting them away. And the worst part is that, on the ride home, Gavin had suggested going by Delvecchio's for candy. But Richard had vetoed the suggestion because he knew he had those chocolate chip cookies at home. But he *doesn't* have those chocolate chip cookies at home. Darnell has gotten to them.

He sighs and hauls himself up the stairs to his room. He passes his older brothers' room and sees Roland is lying on his bed, talking on his cell phone. He's been doing that a lot lately. Richard thinks it must be a girl. Roland salutes him as he goes by, and Richard salutes back.

The only thing that can possibly help him with this disappointment is a few minutes of *Shadow World*. Well, maybe thirty or forty minutes. He needs to relax after walking on eggshells all day around Mr. Blaggart. He can't wait for Ms. Shelby-Ortiz to come back. *How long does the flu last, anyway?* he wonders.

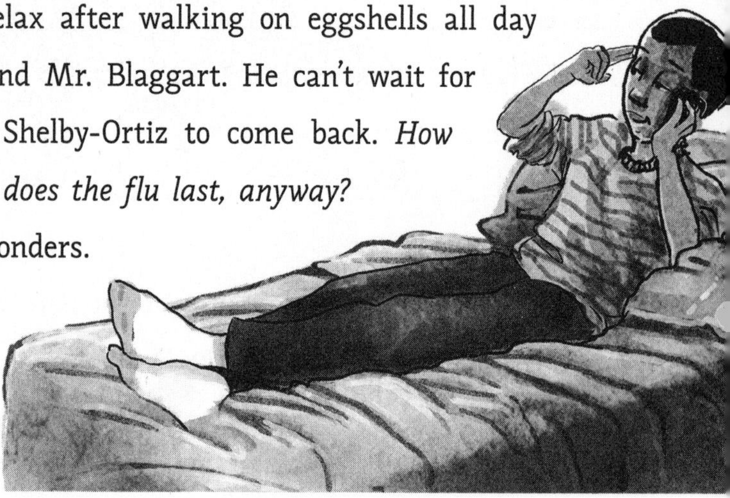

Suddenly, Richard remembers the homework packet. He quickly turns off the video game and gets his backpack, unzips it, and reaches inside. He rummages around for the stapled packet of pages. He doesn't feel it. What's going on? First the cookies, and now his homework? He unzips everything and turns his backpack upside down and gives it several firm shakes. Papers and pencils, the Statue of Liberty book, a peanut butter and jelly sandwich from two weeks ago, pencil shavings, and some random papers fall out onto his floor.

That's it. He has completely ruined it for the class's pizza party! *Where's my packet?* he wonders. *Why isn't it in my backpack?* Then, he can see it clearly. It's on top of the cubbies. He'd placed it up there when he was putting on his sweatshirt. He should have put the packet in his backpack before he put on his sweatshirt. Richard wonders if his mom will be in a good enough mood to take him back to school to get his homework.

○ ○ ○

When he hears his mother's key in the front door, he turns off *Shadow World,* grabs the book on the Statue of Liberty, opens it, and pretends to be reading. He hears the rustle of grocery bags. That sounds promising, but he resists the urge to run down there in hopes of cookies or chips or even graham crackers.

After fifteen minutes or so, he gives up. The thought of chocolate chip cookies pulls him down the stairs and into the kitchen, where his mother is unpacking the groceries.

"There's my boy." She smiles over at him. "What are you up to?"

"Working on my Statue of Liberty paper," he says.

"Oh, right," she says absently. She opens the kitchen cabinet like she's searching for something. "Oops. I was supposed to help you with that, wasn't I?"

"That's okay. I can do it myself." He decides not to tell her that he is actually doing it over because he'd done a lousy job.

"Are there cookies?" he asks after a few moments of silence.

"Not before dinner," she says, dashing his hopes.

He turns to another topic. "Mom, I left my homework packet at school. Can you run me back there to get it?"

"Are you asking me to stop what I'm doing after working all day and take you all the way back to school because you left your homework?"

He nods weakly, already knowing she's going to tell him no.

"I don't think so," she says. "My book club is meeting here tonight, and I have a lot to do."

Richard knows it's no use arguing. When his mother's book club is coming, she can't think of anything else. Not even dinner. She usually orders a couple of pizzas for his father to bring home. So at least there's that. No peas to choke down.

Now he watches her put away a package of cookies in the cabinet above the refrigerator. She still does that, even though Richard and his brothers can easily get the cookies with a stepladder. Jamal can almost get the cookies *without* a stepladder.

"Can I ride my bike back to school and get it? We have a really mean sub, and I don't know what he'll do if I don't turn it in."

His mother stops what she's doing. She looks out the window. She seems to be really considering this. "Okay," she starts slowly. "Keep to the side streets. No talking to strangers and come back with Darnell. He should be finished with 'Homework Club'"—she makes air quotes with her hands—"by then."

"Thanks, Mom!" he says as he dashes out the back door before she can change her mind. *Problem solved!* he thinks.

"And don't forget to wear your helmet!"

● ● ●

Richard gets back to school in no time. He's not surprised to find the gate unlocked. Homework Club is probably just finishing up. The empty, quiet hallways look and feel strange. It's hard to imagine them full of kids and noise. It actually looks kind of sad and lonely.

When he gets to Room Ten, it's locked. He peers through the window in the door, and he can see his homework packet sitting on top of the cubbies, right where he left it. For some reason, he tries the knob again. Still locked, of course. Maybe there's someone

in the office who can help him. He heads back down the hall.

Mrs. Marker is still there, yapping on the telephone. It sounds like school business, so he plops down on the bench just inside the door and waits. Then he grows annoyed at the person on the other end of the call who's keeping Mrs. Marker on the phone. He can tell she's exasperated by the call too. She has to repeat herself several times.

At last, she gets off and looks over her glasses at him. "What is it, Richard?" He's always surprised that she seems to know the names of every kid at Carver Elementary.

He dives in. "I left my homework in the classroom. That's why I came back. To get it."

She frowns. "Why are you telling *me* about *your* homework?"

"The door's locked and I can't get it."

Now she takes in a long breath and lets it out slowly. She shakes her head and shrugs. "I don't have the key. See if you can find the custodian, Mr. Aubrey. He's the only one who can help you."

Richard thanks her and walks out with his shoulders slumped. Mr. Aubrey could be anywhere.

● ● ●

Now Richard walks the hallways, looking through the window of each room. No Mr. Aubrey. He climbs up to the second floor and looks through windows up there. A few teachers are still at their desks. Somehow, he doesn't feel he can interrupt them. They all look kind of tired and like they want to be left alone to do their work.

Homework Club is in the last room he comes to. Before he can look through the window in search of Mr. Aubrey, the door opens and out steps his brother Darnell.

"What are you doing here?"

"Mom let me come back to get my homework. I accidentally left it."

"Did you get it?"

"No. The door is locked."

"So look for the custodian."

"I've been looking and looking and I can't find him. I even asked in the office."

"Well, I'm going home. I'm hungry."

Disappointed, Richard follows his brother to the bike rack. He'll just have to get to school extra early tomorrow. Extra, extra early, then somehow get his homework packet and try to complete it before school and during recess. Because Mr. Blaggart hasn't been checking their homework until after morning recess. It's like he keeps forgetting. Richard thinks he just might be able to pull this off. He really, *really* doesn't want to be the one to ruin it for the class pizza party. He *has* to finish that homework packet.

● ● ●

After dinner, Richard figures he can rewrite those paragraphs on the Statue of Liberty, at least. He flips through the book Mr. Blaggart loaned him and hits upon an idea. Bubble map! He'd forgotten how a bubble map can make a writing assignment easy. Plus, if his mother gets it into her head that she wants to check his progress before the doorbell rings, signaling her first book club member, she'll be impressed.

Richard draws a bubble map and writes The Statue of Liberty Is like a Giant Invitation to the World in the center circle. Then he fills in the other bubbles with everything he can remember about the statue from the book Mr. Blaggart gave him: the expression on her face, the writing on the monument, the way she stands with her arm up, the torch, the crown. All he needs is a topic sentence (ugh) and supporting details (double ugh). It can be done. He gets to work.

Every little thing about how the Statue of Liberty looks makes it look like it's inviting people to America. He scratches out *America* and writes *the United States*. He likes it. It's perfect. But then he scratches out *the United States* and rewrites *America*. He's proud of that topic sentence. He can even be proud to read it the next day. If he has to. It's going to be way different from Antonia's. Way better.

Surprisingly, writing the rest is not as difficult as he thought it would be. When he finishes, he comes up with a plan. He'll show his mother his composition and then quickly ask her if he can go to school the next day extra, *extra* early to get his homework and complete it.

The first book club person will be ringing the doorbell any minute now. He gets to his mom just in time, and pours out his whole speech.

"I don't want you on the street that early," she says. "I'll drive you." Then the bell rings, and she turns toward the front door.

Nine

School in the Early Morning

The next morning, Richard is relieved to see the lighted school office windows and the open front door—open for the early-bird teachers. But then he thinks of Mr. Blaggart and his relief evaporates. That brings on a lot of *what-ifs.*

What if Mr. Aubrey hasn't unlocked the classroom door so Richard can sneak in and get his homework? What if Mr. Blaggart is at school already and sitting at Ms. Shelby-Ortiz's desk, correcting papers or something? Or what if he's already discovered Richard's homework packet and is composing some lecture about responsibility and being a team player?

Richard's shoulders slump as he gets out of the car.

"Good luck," his mother calls to him as he heads up the walkway.

• • •

Richard doesn't stop by the office. He hurries down the hall toward his classroom. The lights are on. He slows. What to do? Dare he look through the window in the door to see if Mr. Blaggart is in there? Before he can decide, the door starts to open. He hurries into the boys' bathroom across the hall from Room Ten just in time. It could be Mr. Aubrey. Maybe he didn't get a chance to sweep the floor the day before, and he's doing it now. Richard opens the restroom door a crack and sees Mr. Blaggart exit the classroom and head toward the teachers' lounge.

This is my chance, Richard thinks. He has to be quick. He scoots across the hall, through his classroom door, and over to the cubbies, and snatches his homework packet off the top. He's out the door in a flash while stuffing the packet in his book bag. What a relief. But suddenly, at the end of the hall, there's Mr. Blaggart, exiting the teachers' lounge, with a steaming cup of something in his hand. He stops.

"Richard?"

Richard swallows. "Hello, Mr. Blaggart."

"What are you doing here so early?"

"Um . . ." He has to think fast. "My mother had to drop me off early." That was kind of true. She *did* have to drop him off early—so he could get his packet and have a chance at getting his homework done.

"I think you know you're not supposed to be in the school building before school starts," Mr. Blaggart says sternly. He seems to be looking at him suspiciously. His eyes settle on the homework packet sticking out of Richard's unzipped backpack. "You want to turn that in?"

Richard follows his gaze. "No . . . I want to— Um, I want to . . ."

"Spit it out," Mr. Blaggart says. "You want to what?"

"I want to check it over first," Richard blurts.

Mr. Blaggart nods slowly with his mouth turned down at the corners. "Well, get to it, then."

Richard hurries down the hall. When he bursts through the double doors leading to the schoolyard, it feels as if he's been let out of detention. He takes a deep breath and jogs over to the lunch tables.

He's able to get the Math worksheets done in record time. It's review: multiplication tables. That's no problem, since his mother made him memorize his multiplication facts all the way to the twelves table. Then there's the three Language Arts worksheet pages on adjectives and the words they're modifying. The instructions are "Underline the adjective once and the word it's modifying twice, then compose five sentences on your own and underline the modified nouns and adjectives." Mr. Blaggart had even added a space for writing a paragraph on a place anywhere in the world that they'd like to visit, and why.

Now, that was going to be a problem. That was going to take time. Richard sighs. How's he going to get everything done?

He looks up to see Nikki and Deja heading his way.

It's too late to get everything into his backpack, away from their prying eyes. Deja seems to speed up as she nears. Before he knows it, she's standing over him with her hands on her hips.

"Are you doing your *homework?* I can't believe it! You're doing your *homework?* You're going to ruin everything for us. You're going to make it so we don't get the pizza party!"

"I accidentally left my homework in the classroom and I tried to get my mom to bring me back here to get it, but she couldn't because—" He stops. Why is he telling all this to *Deja,* anyway? He doesn't owe her an explanation.

"You're going to be the one to make it so we don't have one hundred percent of Room Ten doing everything they're supposed to do."

"Ruin what?" Khufu asks, walking up to them. He's wearing something Richard has seen only old men wear: suspenders. And pants that look too big. Leave it to Khufu.

"I accidentally left my homework packet at school yesterday. So I got here extra, extra early to do it real quick." He looks at Deja. "And I'm almost finished."

Khufu reaches down and turns Richard's paper toward him. "Oh, you only have the paragraph about a place you'd like to visit left to do. Just copy mine and change it a little bit."

"That's cheating," Nikki says in a quiet voice.

Deja looks at Nikki but doesn't say anything. Richard purses his lips. He thinks about Khufu's offer. He really doesn't want to be the one to ruin it for the class. He worried about that all night. Quickly, he reaches for the paper Khufu is now offering him. Time is running out. He has to do it. He has to.

Deja raises an eyebrow. She loops her arm through Nikki's and they walk away. "Glad I did *my* homework" are her parting words.

Richard finishes just as the lineup bell rings. He's still stuffing papers in his backpack as he takes his place.

● ● ●

They wait and wait for Mr. Blaggart, standing tall like soldiers with mouths zipped and eyes straight ahead. While they wait, Rosario rushes up to the line, out of breath and peering at the double doors. She finds her place and says in a not-so-quiet voice to anyone who cares to listen, "Guess what?" But she doesn't wait for a guess. She just dives in. "I saw Mr. Blaggart at Big Barn!"

Without turning around, Deja says, "Are you sure it was him?"

"I'm positive. And he was with a kind of older woman and a little girl."

Looking straight ahead, Antonia, who's in front of Deja, says, "He has a little girl?"

Deja replies, "I think he's too old to have a little girl. I bet it was his granddaughter."

"Or his great-granddaughter," Yolanda adds.

"Or his great-*great*-granddaughter," Nikki whispers.

Then it's all they can do to keep from laughing out loud.

"And the little girl had an ice cream cone," Rosario continues.

"So?" says Deja.

"And it fell onto the floor." Now Rosario has the attention of everyone in the line.

"Then the little girl started to cry. And guess what?"

"Will you just hurry up and tell us?" Antonia says, glancing at the double doors.

"He hurried and got her another cone while the lady cleaned up the mess."

"That couldn't have been Mr. Blaggart, then," Deja states.

"It *was.*"

"I think Mr. Blaggart has a twin," Nikki says.

She looks toward the doors and draws in her mouth while her eyes get big. All the talkers suddenly fall silent and exhibit tiptop line behavior.

• • •

All morning—during journal writing, during silent reading, during workbook activities, during recess—Richard worries. Any minute, Mr. Blaggart is going to get to Khufu's homework. Then he's going to get to Richard's. What's going to happen when he reads their responses to the question *If you could visit anywhere in the world, where would it be and why?* It could mess everything up. Richard glances over at Khufu, who looks like he has no worries. His expression is calm and unreadable as he writes in his workbook.

Khufu had written that he would like to go to Egypt so he could see the place where his name comes from. Richard had written that he would like to go to Egypt so he could see the place where Khufu's name had come from.

That's the problem. Their two topic sentences are practically identical—and everything after that is too similar as well. So it isn't a surprise when Mr. Blaggart looks up from correcting the homework packets and says, "Khufu and Richard . . . come up here, please."

Everyone stops working and watches. Slowly, Richard gets out of his chair. Slowly, he makes his way to Mr. Blaggart, sitting in Ms. Shelby-Ortiz's special chair. Khufu looks nonchalant as he too stands and makes his way over.

"The rest of you can get back to work," Mr. Blaggart says. "This doesn't concern you."

Standing next to Khufu, Richard looks down at

his feet. Then he looks out the window behind Mr. Blaggart, wishing he could be somewhere else. He glances at the desk and sees his and Khufu's papers placed side by side. He swallows.

Mr. Blaggart frowns down at the homework. "I'm going to ask you both a question and I want you to answer me honestly." He turns the two papers so they're facing Richard and Khufu. "I've noticed that your paragraphs are nearly the same." He looks up and studies their faces. "Listen to this. Here's Khufu's response to the question.

"The place I'd like to visit is Egypt. Lots of people want to go to Egypt because they want to see the pyramids and the sphinx and the desert and ride camels and go shopping at the souk. But I want to see it so I can learn about the name Khufu, which is my name. I was named after Khufu, the ancient Egyptian pharaoh who ruled during the Fourth Dynasty. So I'd like to see where that Khufu lived."

"And . . . " Mr. Blaggart continues, drawing it out, "here's yours, Richard."

Richard doesn't want to look at it. He feels tingly all over. Mr. Blaggart begins.

"The place I'd like to visit is Egypt. Lots of people want to go to Egypt because they want to see the pyramids and the sphinx and the desert and ride camels and go shopping at the souk. But I want to see it so I can learn about the name Khufu, which is my friend Khufu's name. He was named after Khufu, the ancient Egyptian pharaoh who ruled during the Fourth Dynasty. So I'd like to see where the real Khufu lived."

Mr. Blaggart glances first at Khufu, then at Richard. "So who wrote the original?" he asks in a calm, even voice.

Richard swallows again. "I copied Khufu's paper," he says quietly. He barely gets it out. He knows this is going to be a big, big problem—not just for him, but for the whole class. He is probably going to lose all his tally marks. And Khufu will, as well. Which means the class's total tally count is going to be below ninety. Which means no pizza party.

"You're both benched for lunch recess," Mr. Blaggart states. "You will each write a new answer to the question. You can get your lunch from the cafeteria if need be and bring it to the classroom, where you will finish the assignment while you eat."

Khufu raises his hand even though he's standing right next to Mr. Blaggart.

"Yes, Khufu."

"Can I still write about Egypt?"

"No."

"But—"

"You'll be writing about a new place."

Khufu returns to his seat.

Almost all the kids are looking at *Richard* as he returns to his seat, too.

That bigmouth Deja. He has a feeling she's behind the looks. He plops down and takes out his notebook. He stares at the blank page and thinks. What can he write about?

Ten

It All Started with Carlos

Richard and Khufu carry their lunch trays into the classroom. Richard looks at the whiteboard and notes that Mr. Blaggart has already erased their points. This, along with Deja's missing point, puts them eleven points down. One point below ninety. Richard's shoulders slump. Nearly a month of perfect lineup behavior down the tubes. It wasn't fair! He didn't leave his homework packet at school on purpose. Things like that happen sometimes. But everyone is going to blame *him*. He pushes his salad around on his cardboard plate, wishing they still sold tater tots in the cafeteria. He stares at his blank notebook page.

He could write about Palm Springs. That was

the last place he and his family went for vacation. It was during spring break and the weather was supposed to be not too hot, but it turned out to be around a hundred fourteen degrees the whole time they were there. He saw a dog under the porch of an old house, trying to keep cool. Boy, was he glad he wasn't a dog trying to keep cool on a one-hundred-fourteen-degree day. The best part about Palm Springs was the hotel they stayed in and, of course, the swimming pool—which he and his brothers practically lived in. He takes a bite out of his turkey burger and begins to write.

After he's finished, he remembers to underline the adjectives once and the nouns twice. Then he remembers to read over what he's written. Ms. Shelby-Ortiz is always telling the class to read over their work before handing it in. So he reads it over and finds a few places where there are missing words. And some sentences that aren't complete thoughts, and some misspellings, too.

Finally, he hands in his work, then finishes his lunch while Khufu is still writing.

• • •

Five minutes before the bell rings, Khufu finally turns in his work and Mr. Blaggart sends them out. "What were you writing about?" Richard asks.

"Paris. I went there with my dad last year. Then I was writing about our case," Khufu says.

Richard is just about to ask him what he means by "our case" when Deja, Antonia, and Rosario run up to them.

"You lost us the pizza party!" Deja says, looking from one to the other. "And we've been working so hard!"

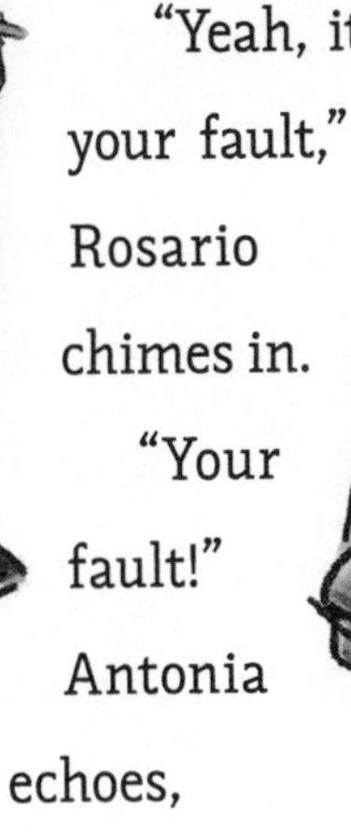

"Yeah, it's all your fault," Rosario chimes in.

"Your fault!" Antonia echoes,

before the three of them turn on their heels and stomp away. Then Deja stops and looks back at Richard. "And the whole class is mad at you, Richard. The *whole class.*"

Richard doesn't know what to say. It *is* his fault. He watches after them for a few moments, then glances over at Khufu, and is surprised to see him looking "calm, cool, and collected." Richard has heard his grandmother use that saying, and he's always wondered what that looked like. Now he knows.

• • •

It's right in the middle of math that Richard realizes this whole thing is actually all Carlos's fault. Yes. Yes! He can trace this right back to *Carlos*. Carlos bringing that stupid triceratops dinosaur to school last week. If Carlos hadn't brought that miniature triceratops dinosaur to school, Richard wouldn't have asked to see it. He wouldn't have had to shove it into his desk when Ms. Shelby-Ortiz passed behind him on her way to the whiteboard to write down their homework assignment. Then, later, when she did a surprise desk check she wouldn't have found that toy and deemed Richard not responsible enough to hang his backpack on his chair.

If that backpack had been on his chair and not in his cubby, he would have put the homework directly into it! But no. Because of Carlos, his backpack was in his cubby, making it super easy to put his packet on top of the cubbies and then forget it when he got distracted by putting on his sweatshirt. Yes. His predicament is all Carlos's fault. Carlos should have left his miniature triceratops dinosaur at home.

It's not the *whole* class that's mad at him. His friends aren't mad. Though everyone *is* kind of quiet on the ride home. Everyone except Khufu (on his ugly orange bike).

"Don't listen to Deja," Khufu says as he drops his bicycle on Richard's front lawn. Gavin and Calvin and Carlos stand astride their bikes.

"Yeah," Gavin says. "She loves making people feel bad."

"Yeah," Calvin and Carlos agree.

Richard could tell them that really the problem began with Carlos bringing that toy to school. And he could explain, step by step, everything that resulted from his bringing in that toy. But Carlos probably wouldn't see it that way, and it would probably make things worse. So he keeps that realization to himself.

His friends ride off and Richard walks his bike to the backyard. He wonders what he will find when he walks into the kitchen. It's been a long day. Will his chocolate chip cookies still be in the vegetable bin, hidden under the carton of organic spinach?

Miracle of miracles. No one is in the kitchen, and the cookies are just where he put them! He grabs one and takes a big bite out of it. He feels better already.

Eleven

The Return of Ms. Shelby-Ortiz

Ms. Shelby-Ortiz is back! During lineup the next morning, Deja tells everyone that she saw Ms. Shelby-Ortiz get out of her car with that big bag she carries and a box of stuff. And she, Deja, got to help her carry her things into the classroom and she, Deja, got to put the date on the board. Not high up though, because she couldn't reach all the way up there and Ms. Shelby-Ortiz wouldn't let her stand on a chair.

"Will you please just shut up?" Antonia demands. "Or do you want Ms. Shelby-Ortiz to catch us not having a perfect line?"

"I just thought the class would want to know that Ms. Shelby-Ortiz is back."

Everyone straightens up even more. Some press

their lips together to keep anything from spilling out.

And then, she's coming toward them. Their dear Ms. Shelby-Ortiz.

Richard's stomach fills up with butterflies as he watches their teacher smile at them, bring her forefinger to her mouth, turn on her heels, and lead them to the classroom.

• • •

Everyone files into Room Ten, with some heading for the cubbies and some heading directly to their tables. The morning journal topic is on the whiteboard. "While Ms. Shelby-Ortiz Was Away." Richard takes out his journal. He suspects that she must know about his part in the class's score falling below ninety points, and now he wonders if she's looking at him differently.

He should have been more mindful of his homework packet. Mr. Blaggart probably told Ms. Shelby-Ortiz about him cheating on his homework assignment, as well. Now she'll see him as irresponsible *and* a cheater. He slowly shakes his head. All those days of standing at attention during morning lineup—and for what? He'd ruined it for the class. They'll probably be talking about this for the rest of the year. He decides to write about the situation in his journal. Then he'll ask to share it.

● ● ●

His hand is the first to go up when Ms. Shelby-Ortiz asks if there is anyone who'd like to share what they've written.

"Okay, Richard," she says. "Please come up to the front of the class."

Once in front of his classmates, he clears his throat. "This is a letter to Ms. Shelby-Ortiz from me, Richard.

"Dear Ms. Shelby-Ortiz, I'm sorry for the class not getting to have the pizza party that they worked so hard to get even though we have two more days left to have a perfect line. But we lost points because of me. I copied Khufu's homework—a part of it—and I lost my points and Khufu lost his points and Deja already lost a point, so . . ."

He's distracted by Deja, who's suddenly waving her hand around and piping up without waiting to be recognized. "Ms. Shelby-Ortiz, it wasn't fair that I lost that point. I forgot to call Mr. Blaggart 'sir' just that one time, and—"

She stops when Ms. Shelby-Ortiz puts her finger to her lips, then says, "We're not discussing that now." She turns to Richard. "Continue, please."

"So I can miss the pizza party. You can send me to Mr. Beaumont's across the hall with some worksheets while everyone has the party. That's all I have to say. Yours truly, Richard."

"Thank you, Richard." Now Ms. Shelby-Ortiz unfolds something that looks like another letter. "I got this from Khufu," she says, "and I'd like the entire class to hear it."

Ms. Shelby-Ortiz begins to read.

"Dear Ms. Shelby-Ortiz, This is Khufu. I'm writing to tell you the truth about me and Richard. He accidentally left his homework packet at school. I personally think this wouldn't have happened if he'd been able to hang his backpack on the back of his chair like most of us—even Carlos."

Ms. Shelby-Ortiz looks puzzled, but continues. "*So I convinced him to let me help him with the thing we had to write about a place he'd like to go to and why. I did this because I felt bad for him. He tried to get all his homework done. He got to school at six thirty when only the office people were at school. And then he got to work and did almost the whole homework packet. I just felt sorry for him and wanted to help, and the only reason he let me help him was so the whole class wouldn't have to suffer because of him. And I felt bad for the class too because they didn't do anything wrong. They were extra good in line for nineteen days and me too. And Richard didn't even want to copy my work. I could tell. Your student, Khufu.*"

As she finishes, Ms. Shelby-Ortiz looks like she's trying to hold back a laugh. The students glance around at each other hopefully, not sure where this is going. Their teacher has another envelope in her hand. Everyone waits, wondering what it is. "This is from Mr. Blaggart," she says finally.

Richard looks around. Almost everyone's eyes are big. Richard knows some are thinking, *Oops! There goes the pizza party.*

Ms. Shelby-Ortiz smiles mysteriously. "I have to admit. I already read this one, too.

"Dear Ms. Shelby-Ortiz, I hope you're feeling better. I've found pomegranate juice builds up the immune system. So here's the bottom line. I had to deduct a few points for this and that, but it wasn't important. You have a good class. Mr. Blaggart. PS: They had excellent lineup behavior the whole time I was here. Just so you know."

"Well," Ms. Shelby-Ortiz goes on, looking around at her students, who are now hanging on her every word, their eyebrows raised. "I am certainly happy about this. But I have to say, I'm not surprised. I *do* have a good class. And we all have to be reminded sometimes to do what we're supposed to do. I have to remind my husband to take the cans to the curb Tuesday evenings for the Wednesday morning trash pickup. The important thing here is: I have a class that tried its best. Richard and Khufu made a mistake, but I know they're sorry." Some of the students glance over at Khufu to see if he looks sorry. "I know they'll do better if they ever find themselves in a similar situation. Soooo . . . Raise your hand if you think Richard and Khufu should join us for our pizza party!"

The boys' hands shoot up. Then Deja's hand shoots up too, and that encourages more and more girls until the whole class has their hands raised. Some are even waving them in the air.

With a big smile, Ms. Shelby-Ortiz walks over to the whiteboard and says, "Okay, then. Let's vote. What kind of pizza do we all want?"

Read more about the kids of Carver Elementary!

Karen English is a Gryphon Award winner, a Coretta Scott King Honor recipient, and the author of the Nikki & Deja series, as well as the Carver Chronicles. Her chapter books have been praised for their accessible writing, authentic characters, and satisfying story lines. She is a former elementary school teacher and lives with her husband in Los Angeles, California.

Laura Freeman has illustrated several books for children, including all twelve of the chapter books about the kids of Carver Elementary. She grew up in New York City and now lives near Atlanta, Georgia, with her husband and two sons. Her drawings for this book were inspired by her children, as well as her own childhood.